SLEEPOVER ZOO

Brenda Kearns

Library and Archives Canada Cataloguing in Publication

Kearns, Brenda, 1963-, author
        Sleepover zoo / Brenda Kearns.

Originally published: Richmond Hill, Ont. : Scholastic Canada, ©1998.
ISBN 978-1-927711-03-3 (pbk.)

        I. Title.

PS8571.E355S53 2014   jC813'.54   C2014-907651-7

Also by Brenda Kearns:

Home

The Day I Washed My Face in the Toilet

There's Nothing Wrong With Claudia

Parrots and Popcorn

Ediciones en español:

El día que me lavé la cara en el inodoro

Fiesta de pijamas en el zoológico

No hay nada malo con Claudia

Pericos y palomitas de maíz

Éditions françaises:

Le Jour où je me suis lavé la figure dans la cuvette

Pyjamazoo

Claudine ne fait jamais rien de mal

Pop-corn et perroquets

For my wonderful kids — my favorite people.

Table of Contents

Chapter 1: Lunch bag surprise 7

Chapter 2: It's just not normal! 10

Chapter 3: Giant dogs and frozen mice.......................15

Chapter 4: Parrots shouldn't drink coffee 20

Chapter 5: Your backpack is moving........................ 24

Chapter 6: Snake in a box... 27

Chapter 7: Catching the flu 30

Chapter 8: A sleepover she'll never forget................. 34

Chapter 9: Big birds and little earrings 40

Chapter 10: She'll be back 44

Chapter 11: Real friends... 48

Chapter 12: Mortimer likes you! 52

Chapter 1

LUNCH BAG SURPRISE

"*What* is *that?*" yelled Leona. Everyone in the lunchroom looked up.

Toni's face turned red. She had tried to drop the bag of tiny brown seeds into her lap, but Leona had seen her do it. Now everyone was looking. "They're flax seeds," she mumbled. "I got the wrong lunch."

Toni shuffled in her seat, but everyone still stared. I guess this is what it's like to be the new kid, she thought to herself. She peeked into her lunch bag and sighed. The sandwich was at the bottom. She'd have to empty everything else out first.

"My dad sometimes takes food for the birds where he works," said Toni. She pulled out a bag of sunflower seeds, then another of pumpkin seeds. A third bag had shredded coconut inside. She reached in again and brought out a brown, mushy banana. Its insides were oozing out.

Lunch couldn't get any worse than this.

Finally, Toni pulled out the sandwich. It had a big dent in the middle, and most of the peanut butter and jelly had squished out the sides.

Okay, so it could get worse.

"That's gross!" said Leona. Her friends giggled.

Toni had only been at Renforth Elementary for three weeks, but she already knew enough about Leona Sharp. When Leona talked, the other kids listened. When she threw a party — like her giant sleepover two weeks ago — *all* the girls in the class were expected to show up.

Leona twirled one of her brand-new gold stud earrings and grinned at Toni. "So, Toni, when are you having a sleepover?" asked Leona. "I want to see that bird house you live in."

"She doesn't live in a bird house." Meghan Brady sat down beside Toni and straightened her glasses. "Her parents run the Wild Bird Care Center. They take *care* of birds."

Toni smiled at Meghan, then looked down at her lunch. Meghan had put a chocolate chip cookie beside Toni's mushed-up sandwich.

"Thanks," whispered Toni. Meghan was her first new friend at Renforth. They'd promised to always eat lunch together.

"But you came to *my* party," said Leona. "When are you having yours?" She leaned in toward Toni. "I want to see this bird house!"

Meghan frowned. "She doesn't live in a..."

—

"Friday," said Toni. "I'm having a sleepover on Friday. And it isn't a bird house, Leona."

Leona glared at Toni. "So who else is coming?"

"I...um..." Toni cleared her throat. "I'll have to ask my parents. I don't know how many I can invite."

Toni frowned as she walked back to class. She had hoped that Leona would just ignore her, but it looked like she wasn't going to. Now Leona wanted to come over to her house! What if she thought it was really weird? She'd make such a big deal out of it!

"Hey! Wait up!" called Meghan. "Are you really having a sleepover Friday?"

"I guess so. If my parents will let me. But I shouldn't have opened my big mouth. I don't really want Leona there."

Meghan shrugged. "Leona's stuck up," she said. "Anyway, I'd like to come. You still haven't shown me the Bird Care Center. I mean, it can't be *that* bad!"

Toni sighed. If Meghan was going to be Toni's friend, she'd have to see the birds sooner or later. "Well, I have to do chores after school. It's boring, but you can come if you want."

"Thanks! Maybe I can help."

Toni smiled at Meghan's white sweater, new jeans and neatly braided hair. Meghan never got dirty.

"You'll need to wear my old jeans if you want to help. And you'll need gloves for the dead mice, too."

Meghan gasped. "Dead *mice*?"

"Well, it could be worse," said Toni, trying not to laugh. "If they were alive, you'd have to catch them!"

Chapter 2

IT'S JUST NOT NORMAL!

After lunch, Mr. Wentworth gave the class a surprise math quiz. Toni couldn't concentrate.

Why does Leona have to come over? she kept thinking to herself. She doesn't want to be friends with me. She's probably just being nosy.

Maybe Mom will say Friday is too soon, she thought. No. She'd already said Toni could have friends over any time.

Maybe Leona won't be allowed to come on Friday. No. Meghan said Leona went to *all* the sleepovers!

"Antonina Maria Amadeo! How long are you going to stare at that paper?"

Toni jumped and dropped her pencil. Why did Mr. Wentworth have to use her full name? Toni wondered. Every time he did, all the boys laughed.

"Sorry, Mr. Wentworth," mumbled Toni.

Toni looked down at her quiz. She'd only finished half the questions.

Mr. Wentworth glanced at her paper and frowned. "Antonina Maria! Is something bothering you?"

"Um...no," said Toni. There was no point in telling Mr. Wentworth. He couldn't help.

The rest of the day took forever. Toni made so many mistakes on her spelling sheet that she had to ask for a new one. By the time she had picked a topic for her art project, there was no time left to start working on it.

When the bell rang, Meghan jumped out of her seat. "Come on! You have to show me the birds!"

As they pulled on their coats, Leona and three of her friends walked past. Leona turned to Toni with a dazzling smile. "Friday, right?" she said. She didn't wait for an answer, though. The four of them kept walking. They whispered to each other as they disappeared down the hall.

Shaking her head, Meghan grabbed Toni's arm and pulled her toward the school doors.

"You don't *really* have dead mice, do you?" she asked.

"Just wait and see!" Toni grinned.

A sleepover would be fun — as long as the birds behaved, and as long as Leona liked them, and as long as Leona didn't tell the whole world about Toni's house...

She sighed. This really was a nightmare.

Outside, the sun bounced off the ice and snow and made Toni's eyes water. She squinted and pulled her scarf over her cold cheeks.

Hey! Let's ice-walk down your street!" yelled Meghan.

They turned onto Montcalm Drive and climbed to the top of a snow bank. The lawns below were covered with a deep layer of sparkling white snow. Most of the snowdrifts were higher than the fences.

Best of all, for as far as Toni could see, the snow was covered with ice. If it was thick enough, it would be perfect for ice-walking! And Montcalm Drive had the *best* ice-walking!

"You go first," said Meghan.

Toni gingerly stepped onto the first slippery, ice-covered lawn. Then she jumped as a huge snowball smashed into her shoulder. Bruno! He was walking on the other side of the road.

Bruno always said that because he was her brother he could call Toni names. He figured that because he was fifteen he could boss her around and tease her. But sometimes he took the blame so she wouldn't get in trouble, and he always helped her with math homework. Bruno was okay.

"Hey, brat! Finally bringing Meghan home?"

"Yup. You know Leona Sharp? She wants to sleep over Friday night."

Bruno laughed as he threw another snowball. Toni ducked, and the snowball smashed into a maple tree.

"Good luck," said Bruno. "She sounds like a snob."

"What will you tell your parents?" asked Meghan. She slipped her foot forward to test the ice.

"I don't know," said Toni. "Leona *can't* see the Bird

Care Center. She doesn't have any pets, and her house is so...well, you know."

At Leona's party, their sleeping bags had been spread out in a neat row on the floor of her huge bedroom. All of her toys were lined up perfectly on the bookshelf, and all of her shoes were in a perfect row in the closet!

There were no pets, no dust balls, no dirty dishes and no fingerprints anywhere. It was so clean, it was almost spooky.

Leona had made sure it stayed that way, too. She had one of those mini vacuum cleaners in her room, and when anything got dropped, she cleaned it up right away. Leona had even washed all their dishes right after the movie, and her mom had ironed all their pillowcases before they went to sleep. Toni had never seen such a perfect house.

"Well, I think you should have the sleepover. If Leona doesn't like your house, she doesn't have to come back."

"Yeah, but still..." muttered Toni. "Hey, wait a minute!" She turned so fast that she almost lost her balance. "My dad's still finishing the kitchen cupboards! A lot of the kitchen stuff is in boxes. Maybe he'll say no because of that!"

A snowball hit the back of Toni's neck.

"Bruno!" she yelled.

"Sorry, squirt. I was aiming for your head!"

Meghan laughed as she climbed the first icy snowdrift. She crouched down low and walked with tiny shuffling steps. "You know," she said. "I don't think Leona would care about a few boxes."

"Oh, Meghan, it isn't just that," said Toni. "Our basement is full of birds. I've got a worm farm in my room, and there are feathers *everywhere*. It's just not normal!"

"Hey, brat! Don't forget the snake that got out of its cage last week. It could be anywhere!"

"You lost a *snake*?" yelled Meghan. "Why didn't you tell me you...OOMPH!"

Toni looked over her shoulder. Meghan had disappeared, but the top of her hat poked through a large hole in the snow.

Toni tried not to laugh as she slid over to the hole. When Meghan stood up, she was shoulder-deep in snow.

"You lost a *snake*?" yelled Meghan. She wiped the snow off her face and shook out her hat.

"We'll find it soon." Toni helped Meghan climb out of the hole. "It's somewhere in the house. Snakes won't go outside when it's this cold. Come on. I'll show you the birds."

"You lost a *snake*!" Meghan wiped off her glasses and brushed the snow out of her hair.

Bruno laughed. "I think Meghan will like our place!"

Chapter 3

GIANT DOGS AND FROZEN MICE

When they got home, Toni propped their wet boots over the heating vent. Meghan wiped the frost off her glasses, then stared down the hall. "That's a dog?"

"That's Duke," said Toni. "He's a Great Dane."

At the sound of his name, Duke stood up and stretched. He was light brown, and he was taller than the hall table.

"He weighs more than my dad. He's huge, isn't he? Meghan?"

"Look at that!" Meghan was pointing into the living room.

"That's Mortimer," said Bruno. "We rescued him. He's a blue-and-yellow macaw. That's a type of parrot."

Mortimer had pulled a newspaper onto the couch and

shredded it to make a huge, fluffy nest.

"He does that all the time," said Toni. "Come on! I'll show you the mess in the kitchen. My dad will say no to a sleepover for sure!"

Bruno got there first. "Hey kid, just wait till you see this!"

Toni ran into the kitchen. The cupboards were done. Every single one. There wasn't a box anywhere. Toni's heart sank.

"Well runt, looks like Dad got finished today. Hey! My koi!"

Bruno dropped his coat and ran across the kitchen to the big aquarium. A tiny kitten was leaning over the side of the tank, splashing the water with its front paws. Bright red and yellow fish, bigger than the kitten, darted around the tank.

"That's Avery. He's eight weeks old," said Toni, as Bruno grabbed the orange kitten and dropped him onto the floor. "He's been trying to catch the koi ever since Bruno brought him home. Would you like some lemonade?"

"I...uh...sure." Meghan was watching Avery slide across the kitchen floor. He was soaking wet. "What's a koi?"

"They're a fancy type of fish — they look kind of like goldfish but they can grow up to three feet long. People in Japan say koi are lucky and can bring you friendship." Toni stepped over Avery. He was drying himself off on Bruno's coat.

Toni poured two tall glasses of lemonade, while Meghan wiped a pile of bird feathers off the table.

"Oh, Meghan, what am I going to do?" asked Toni. "I

could just say my mom won't let me have a sleepover..."

"But that isn't true. Besides, you know Leona's going to keep bugging you about it. Why not get it over with?"

"She's right, you know." Bruno pulled his coat out from under Avery and stomped down the basement stairs. "Face your fears!" he called out.

Toni frowned. They didn't understand. Bruno's friends thought the Bird Care Center was great, and Meghan had lived in Renforth all her life. Nobody made a fuss about her.

"I don't know anyone yet, Meghan. I don't want Leona telling stories about me." Toni handed Meghan her lemonade. "I know! I'll get sick!"

"But Friday's only two days away. She'll know you're faking it." Meghan watched as Avery clawed his way up the curtains and jumped to the window ledge by her head. He crawled toward the aquarium, twitching his tail to keep his balance.

"Hey! I'll say my mom and dad are having company."

"Leona will tell everyone you cancelled out."

Avery leaped off the ledge and tried to grab on to the edge of the aquarium. But he missed and landed in Duke's water dish, instead.

Meghan laughed so hard she choked on her lemonade. Clearing her throat, she said, "Can I see the birds now?"

Toni took a deep breath. This was it.

When they got to the bottom of the stairs, Meghan's mouth fell open. Toni glanced around the room while she waited for Meghan to say something.

It looked like a library, except that the shelves were

closed in with wire screen to make cages. Pails and brooms and boxes were piled in the middle of the room, and green garbage bags filled with leaves and branches lay open by the cages.

Feathers covered everything, and the noise of the birds filled the room. Bruno was in the corner pouring a huge bag of sunflower seeds into a storage bin.

"Wow! I didn't think it would look like this!" Meghan had to raise her voice to be heard over the squawks and cheeps.

"My mom and dad work at the Renforth Animal Shelter during the day. They don't have room there for wild birds, so we keep the sick ones here until they can be set free." Toni picked up a box of gauze that had fallen off the medicine shelf. "We did the same thing at our old house."

Meghan walked slowly around the room, peering into each cage. "Is that a sparrow?"

"Yes. A house sparrow, actually." Toni touched the cage, and the tiny brown bird hopped behind a branch. "She flew into a window and broke her wing."

Suddenly, a high-pitched scream burst across the room.

Meghan gasped and stumbled backward. She tripped over a broom and fell into an open bag of leaves.

"What was *that*?" she asked.

"That's a red-tailed hawk." Toni pointed toward a large cage in the corner. "His leg was broken in a hunter's trap. We'll be releasing him in about a month."

The huge brown-and-white bird slowly turned its back to them and fanned out its rust-colored tail. Then it turned to face Meghan and screamed again.

"Well, he isn't very friendly," said Meghan, wiping the leaves off her jeans.

Bruno rolled his eyes. "They're wild animals, not pets. If we tamed them, they couldn't go back in the wild." He grabbed a garbage can and dragged it toward the cages. "Come on, squirt. It's almost time for dinner."

"All he does is eat," Toni whispered to Meghan. She pulled on a pair of old leather gloves and gently lifted a tiny chickadee out of its cage. Bruno rolled up the dirty newspapers and quickly washed the walls and floor of the pen.

When he had finished, Bruno looked at his watch. "We're supposed to be starting dinner," he said. "You two clean out the hawk's cage and then get the blueberries out of the freezer." At the sound of Bruno's voice, the hawk screamed again.

Meghan backed away and straightened her glasses. "I'll get the blueberries."

"What a chicken," Bruno mocked, as he spread out a fresh sheet of newspaper and sprinkled it with leaves. "She just doesn't want to get dirty!"

Meghan looked at the two freezers, then lifted the lid of the bigger one. Bruno grinned at Toni.

"You know," he whispered, "you should have warned her about the frozen mice."

"*AAAIIIGGGHHH!*" screamed Meghan.

Chapter 4

PARROTS SHOULDN'T DRINK COFFEE

"Mice!"

Meghan shuddered and backed away from the freezer.

"Oh, Meghan, I'm sorry," said Toni. "I forgot to tell you — we keep *our* food in the small freezer."

Bruno was laughing so hard he collapsed onto the floor. "What did you think we feed the owls and hawks...donuts?"

"Stop it, Bruno," said Toni. "Are you okay, Meghan?"

"I guess so," said Meghan. She wiped her hands on her jeans and straightened her sweater. "I'd better get home, though. I'm probably late for dinner."

Bruno laughed. "Don't be a goof! They're only mice!"

"I'd like to see Leona touch one!" Meghan gasped.

Toni groaned. She'd been so busy she'd forgotten all about the sleepover...Hey! That was it! She'd *forget* to ask her parents. Then the sleepover would have to be cancelled. They'd never agree to it at the last minute!

As Toni waved goodbye to Meghan, her parents drove up the driveway.

"Good luck! Tell me all about it tomorrow!" Meghan called from the street.

When Toni sat down for dinner, Mortimer the parrot hopped across the table and stood waiting beside her placemat. Toni rolled her eyes at him and dropped a piece of potato on the table. Mortimer jumped on it.

Toni smiled. Who cares if Mortimer has rotten table manners? she thought. I'll just forget to ask about the sleepover and Leona won't be able to come over. Then maybe she'll forget about the whole thing!

Bruno slopped applesauce on his third pork chop. "Hey Dad, did Toni ask you about — "

Toni kicked him under the table. Hard.

Bruno looked at her and grinned. "Well? Did you ask them yet?"

Toni glared at Bruno, but he wasn't looking at her anymore. He was feeding Mortimer a pickle. She tried to kick him again, but he'd moved his leg.

"What's up, Antonina?" her father asked.

"Um..." Toni coughed. "Can I have a sleepover Friday night?"

Please say no. Please say no. Please say no, Toni thought.

"Sure," said her father. "I've finally got the kitchen cupboards done, so it's no problem."

Toni sighed and turned to her mother. "I can only have one friend, right? Not two?"

Please say one. Please say one. Please say one, she thought.

"Two is fine, Antonina. You can put your sleeping bags in the living room."

"You get to sleep with Mortimer and Duke and Avery!" Bruno laughed as Mortimer dragged the pork chop off of Toni's plate.

"Could we have pizza and ice cream? Please? Just this once?" Toni asked.

Please say yes. Please say yes. Please say yes, she thought.

"Oh, Antonina. You know we always have fish sticks on Fridays. You love them."

There was nothing more to say. Soon Leona would be telling everyone what it was like at Toni's house. What a mess.

Mortimer flew to the counter and landed beside the coffee maker. He stared at the coffee pot and made clicking sounds with his beak.

"Why so quiet, Antonina?" Toni's father walked to the counter and poured a cup of coffee. Mortimer flew back to the table and waited by the sugar bowl.

"Leona will think we're weird."

"Why would she think that?" Toni's father set the cup of coffee beside Mortimer and stirred in a huge spoonful of sugar.

"Because I have a worm farm in my room, Mortimer takes food off our plates, the basement is full of birds and...and we never eat good food."

Toni swallowed hard and stared at her plate. No one spoke. Bruno and Mortimer were the only ones still eating. Mortimer grabbed his cup with one foot and slowly lapped up the coffee with his thick black tongue.

"And parrots shouldn't drink coffee," Toni muttered.

"Antonina, I'm sorry if our home embarrasses you, but we've made a promise to take care of these birds," said her father. "And there's nothing I can do about Mortimer. He just isn't himself without his coffee."

Toni looked glumly at Mortimer. Coffee was dripping off his beak and running down his belly. He had a piece of pickle stuck between his toes.

They finished their dinner in silence. Toni pushed the green beans around her plate. What else could go wrong?

Chapter 5

YOUR BACKPACK IS MOVING

"Now, class, this is *silent* reading. Your book report is due on Friday — and that's tomorrow. So get moving!"

Mr. Wentworth was in a bad mood. All the students quietly read their books. Even Leona stopped whispering.

Toni read the same sentence three times. She couldn't concentrate.

"Psssst!" Toni looked up. Meghan was peeking back over her shoulder.

"What?" Toni whispered.

"What did your dad say?"

"He said yes," Toni whispered.

"What?"

"He said *yes.*"

"Antonina Maria Amadeo!" called Mr. Wentworth. "Would you like to share your conversation with the rest of the class?"

"No, Mr. Wentworth. Sorry."

"Then keep reading," he said.

Toni looked down at her book and chewed her lip. Her heart was pounding and her face felt hot.

When it was time for gym class, Toni still hadn't finished the first chapter of her book. She grabbed her backpack and headed for the gym with Meghan.

"Hey, wait up!" called Leona, as she hurried to catch up to them.

This is it, thought Toni. This is my last chance to get out of this. But how?

"My mom says I can go to your sleepover. Is it still on for Friday?" asked Leona.

"I guess so."

"Great! I hope we're having pizza. See you later!"

Leona twirled one of her earrings as she walked back to her group of friends.

Meghan looked at Toni. "Stop frowning. It'll work out okay."

"What do I do now?" Toni threw her backpack over her shoulder and scowled. "My dad said no pizza and ice cream, and Leona's going to hate sleeping in a *bird* house." In the changing room, Toni dropped her backpack on the bench. "She won't understand anything about the Bird Care Center."

Meghan straightened her glasses and emptied her gym bag. "Oh, yuck! I forgot to put my shirt in the laundry. *Look* at it!" Meghan held out her white T-shirt.

Toni laughed. No one but Meghan would be so mad about a wrinkled gym shirt. Her clothes were always neat.

"If you don't like that," said Toni, "it's a good thing you didn't clean the bird cages! *Then* you'd be dirty!"

"Um, Toni..." said Meghan.

"Besides, it's just a gym shirt!"

"Toni..."

"Hey, I've got it! Mortimer's old cage is in the basement. I'll just put him down there and lock the basement door. Then all she'll see is Duke and Avery. What do you think?"

"TONI!" yelled Meghan.

"What?"

"Your backpack is moving," said Meghan.

Suddenly, the room got very quiet. Everyone turned to look at Toni's backpack. It *was* moving. The bottom end was bulging out and sinking back in.

Leona walked into the changing room just as Toni opened her backpack.

Please don't be Mortimer. Please don't be Mortimer. Please don't be Mortimer, Toni begged.

When nothing happened, she lifted her backpack from the bottom and emptied it onto the bench.

Leona screamed and ran into the corner. The rest of the class followed her.

It wasn't Mortimer. It was the lost snake.

Chapter 6

SNAKE IN A BOX

"What's going on in here?" Mrs. Lee, the principal stood in the doorway of the changing room and stared at Toni.

Toni looked around the room. Gym clothes were scattered across the floor. Meghan was sitting on the bench trying not to laugh, and everyone else was crammed into the farthest corner.

Toni held onto the snake — it was longer than her arm — and tried to think of what to say.

"Antonina! What are you doing with that snake?" asked Mrs. Lee.

"It was in my backpack, Mrs. Lee. I don't know how it got there. I didn't do it on purpose!" Toni's face felt so hot that it burned.

"Meghan, stop giggling," said Mrs. Lee. "And the rest of you, pick up your clothes and get ready for gym. That snake is harmless."

Meghan took off her glasses and wiped her eyes. The rest of the class looked doubtful.

"Now, I want you girls to hurry up. You're going to be late for class. Antonina, come with me." Mrs. Lee stomped out of the changing room.

Toni held up the snake so she wouldn't trip on it. When she caught up to Mrs. Lee, Toni peeked at her face.

Mrs. Lee was laughing! Her shoulders were shaking, her cheeks were red and her eyes were watering!

"Oh, Antonina," Mrs. Lee said, when she saw Toni staring at her. "I've been at Renforth for 15 years, and this is the first time a student has brought a snake to school by *accident!*"

Mrs. Lee found a cardboard box and punched air holes in the top. She tried not to smile as Toni put her snake in the box.

"Do I have to feed this thing, or will it be okay until you take it home?" she asked.

"It'll be okay. Thanks, Mrs. Lee."

"Go back to gym. And don't forget to take your snake home tonight!"

When Toni got back to the gym, warm-ups were almost finished. She changed quickly and got in line with the rest of the girls.

They had just started the obstacle course. Meghan was taking her turn, and Leona was next in line. Leona backed up until she was standing beside Toni.

"Did you get a detention?" asked Leona.

"No."

"Didn't you get in trouble?"

"Not really. Mrs. Lee just put the snake in a box and said to take it home after school. She thought it was funny."

"You're lucky! If that's what your house is like, it'll be a weird sleepover."

Toni felt her face grow hot. "It was an accident, Leona. Besides, my house isn't weird, it's just...*different*." Toni's chest felt tight and her eyes burned. "It'll be the best sleepover — ever!"

"What are you so mad about? I was only joking." Leona laughed and ran to the start of the obstacle course. Everyone watched her. She would get the best score — she always did.

"Your face is all red," said Meghan, as she got in line behind Toni. "What did Leona say?"

"She said it was going to be a weird sleepover."

Meghan rolled her eyes. "What did you say?"

"I told her it would be the best one ever." Toni shook her head. "I should have kept my mouth shut."

Meghan laughed softly. "Well, it'll be a sleepover she'll never forget!"

Toni groaned. "That's what I'm afraid of."

Chapter 7

CATCHING THE FLU

"Thanks for finding my snake," said Bruno, as he grabbed another grilled cheese sandwich. "I owe you one."

"Help me get out of this sleepover, then." Toni lifted her feet out of the way so Duke could crawl under the table. Avery scurried past him and hopped up beside the fish tank.

"I had friends over last week, Toni. It's no big deal," said Bruno. "Besides, Leona's going to see the place eventually. Why not get it over with?"

Avery stood on his tiny hind legs, smacking his paw at the fish behind the aquarium glass. When Duke heard the noise, he stood up and lifted the kitchen table right off the floor.

"Duke, down!" yelled Toni, as the salad bowl tipped over and an apple rolled into her lap. With a grunt, Duke lay down.

As Toni reached for her napkin, Mortimer flew over to the table and skidded to a stop beside her plate.

"Oh, Bruno, what will Leona say if she sees this place?"

"Just keep her in the living room." Bruno pulled Avery off the edge of the aquarium, then grabbed the last grilled cheese sandwich.

Toni cleared her throat. "I want to put Mortimer downstairs in his cage. Just for one night. Then I can lock the basement door and Leona will never see the birds."

Bruno snorted and shook his head. "Wake up, runt. Dad put a blue jay in Mortimer's cage last week, and there's never *been* a lock on the basement door."

Bruno stirred sugar into Mortimer's coffee. "Besides, Mortimer can't miss dinner. You know he just isn't himself without his coffee."

Mortimer hopped onto the rim of his coffee cup to take a drink, but he lost his balance. Coffee splashed across the table as the parrot scrambled up and flew away.

Toni groaned. Salad was scattered across the table and coffee was dripping onto the floor.

Bruno scraped the salad back into the bowl, then stood up and put the bowl on the counter. "You get the coffee. I think the neighbor's cat is scratching at the door again."

Toni sighed as she mopped up the mess and poured Mortimer another cup of coffee. No pizza, no ice cream and a ton of birds. Some sleepover.

The front door slammed. Bruno stalked into the

kitchen.

"That dumb cat," he muttered. "That's the fifth bird he's killed since we got here. I wish he'd quit leaving them on our doorstep."

"He's outside all the time — maybe he has to get his own food," said Toni. "After all, Avery never attacks our birds."

Bruno grunted. He kicked off his boots and went to wash his hands.

Then Toni had an idea. Her father always bought groceries on Fridays. Maybe he was secretly planning something special for the sleepover. Toni searched the refrigerator door, but the grocery list was gone.

"Give up, shrimp," Bruno said, as he dropped into his chair. "If Dad wanted to surprise you, he wouldn't just leave the grocery list lying around." He gulped down his milk and refilled the glass.

Toni frowned. Duke was still lying under the table. When he saw her looking at him, his tail thumped happily on the floor.

"Good boy, Duke," Toni muttered.

Duke jumped up and headed toward Toni, but the table caught on his back. Bruno grabbed his plate and the milk jug.

"No, Duke, *down*!" Bruno yelled. Newspapers slid off the table and scattered across the floor. "Nice going, twerp!"

Toni leaned down to pick up the mess. The grocery list! It had been under the newspapers.

As Toni quickly read the list, her heart sank. There was no pizza and no ice cream. Not even a bottle of soda. Even worse, her dad was buying fish sticks.

"I am *not* having Leona here," said Toni. Bruno just shrugged.

The sleepover isn't until tomorrow night, she thought. I can catch the flu by then.

That night, after she had changed into her pajamas, Toni opened her bedroom window — all the way. Fluffy snowflakes drifted into the room.

She breathed in the cold air and shivered. You can catch the flu by getting a chill, she thought. I'll be sick by tomorrow for sure!

Chapter 8

A SLEEPOVER SHE'LL NEVER FORGET

Toni peeked out her window. They'll be here any minute, she thought. There's no way I can hide this.

Toni gathered up the wet towels and threw them on her bed. What a mess. The rug was soaked, the curtains were soaked, and the wallpaper under her window had peeled off.

It was bad enough that she had woken up freezing that morning, with her bed covered in snow. But then Mr. Wentworth had given them another surprise math quiz. And now a soaking wet room. And she didn't even have a sore throat — not even a runny nose!

Bruno picked up the worm farm and carried it down the hall. "What were you thinking?" he shouted. "You could have killed your plants. You could have wrecked the worm farm. You could have caught the *flu...*"

Bruno's voice faded as he marched down the basement stairs with the dirt-filled barrel.

Toni grabbed her glue stick and smeared some glue onto the back of the loose strip of wallpaper. She tried to push the paper flat against the wall, but every time she let go it dropped to the floor again.

"Give me *one* good reason why I shouldn't tell Mom." Bruno was back. He was standing in the doorway with a jar of wallpaper paste and a paintbrush.

Toni grabbed her fern and shook the water off it. "Because last night you said you owed me."

Bruno scowled as he spread paste on the wall. "You should have told me about this before we left for school. It'll still be wet when Meghan and Leona get here."

Toni frowned. "It doesn't really matter. Leona's only coming to see the birds." She shooed Mortimer away from the open jar of wallpaper paste. "Besides, I didn't know the snow would *melt.*"

Bruno rolled his eyes and shook his head as he smoothed the paper over the sticky wall. "What did you expect? There's a heating vent under your window." Then he stood up and looked out the window. "Meghan's coming up the driveway."

Toni ran to the door. Snow swirled into the living room as Meghan shook off her boots and stomped in.

"Look!" Meghan dropped her backpack and opened her coat. "I even dressed for chores!" She was wearing faded jeans and an old sweater. "Did you know there's a cat climbing up your bird feeder?" she asked.

Bruno raced to the door and yanked it open. "Leona's here," he muttered, as he struggled into his boots.

Toni held open the screen door as Bruno ran out and Leona scurried in.

"Hi," said Leona, as she watched Bruno chase the cat down the driveway. "What's *he* doing?"

"He's trying to scare our neighbor's cat away from the feeder. It's been killing the sparrows," said Toni.

Leona wrinkled her nose. "I saw a cat kill a bird last summer. It was disgusting."

Meghan raised her eyebrows as Leona pulled off her coat. "You look, umm...nice, Leona."

Leona was wearing a brand-new purple dress and shiny gold earrings. She had a gold scrunchie in her hair.

Leona looked at Meghan's jeans and frowned. "Well, I didn't want to look like a *slob*!" She lifted her head and sniffed. "*What* is that smell?"

"It's the birds," said Toni.

Leona made a face and fiddled with her earrings. "They stink. Why don't you keep them outside?"

"They're hurt," said Bruno, as he pulled off his boots. "Most of them aren't strong enough to survive really cold or hot weather yet."

"Hmph." Leona looked bored and straightened her ponytail. "Well, what are we doing first? You have to show me this bird house, you know."

Meghan rolled her eyes. "You're not exactly dressed for it, Leona. Besides, it's not a — "

Suddenly, the floor shook. Duke galloped into the room and ran straight to Leona. He wagged his tail as he licked her face and hair with his big wet tongue.

Leona staggered backward and tried to cover her face. "Help me! Get him off me!"

"Duke, *no!*" yelled Toni.

Duke spun around and trotted into the kitchen with Leona's scrunchie dangling from his teeth.

Leona scrambled to her feet. Her dress was wrinkled and her hair and face were wet.

"Oh, *yuck!* What was *that?*" Leona yelled, wiping frothy dog drool off her face.

"That's Duke!" said Meghan. "I guess he likes scrunchies!"

Bruno laughed. "Didn't want to look like a slob, eh? Come on — you wanted to see the birds."

Meghan grinned as she followed Toni and Bruno into the basement. For once, Leona had nothing to say. She frowned and stomped down the stairs behind them.

When Leona reached the bottom of the stairs, her mouth dropped open. "How...why...?" She closed her mouth and shook her head.

"They're all injured or sick," said Toni. "We keep them until they can go back to the wild."

Toni wanted to get Leona out of the basement fast, but Bruno started filling the water bowls.

Meghan walked around a pile of empty moving boxes and stopped at the first row of cages. "Wow, I didn't even look over here yesterday. What's this one?" She pointed to a huge gray-colored owl with a black spot on its chin.

"That's a great gray owl," said Toni.

"WHOO! WHOO! WHOO!" it boomed. Avery jumped and pulled back his ears. He knocked over the brooms as he scurried away from the cage.

"He's too loud!" said Leona, covering her ears.

Meghan rolled her eyes. "What's wrong with him?"

"Intestinal parasites," said Bruno.

Leona stared at Bruno. "Intestinal what?"

"Parasites," said Toni. "He had a tapeworm in his belly. Bruno dewormed him, and when he gains some weight, we can set him free."

As Toni spoke, the owl hopped off its perch and picked at its dinner.

"Yuck! What's he eating?" asked Leona, backing away from the cage.

Meghan laughed. "It's a mouse! There are lots in the freezer, if you're hungry."

Leona glared at Meghan. "That's sick!"

Meghan shrugged and then pointed to one of the top cages. "What are those?" Two green-and-orange birds were huddled side by side on a branch.

"They're baby lovebirds. When they're old enough, we have to find a home for them." Toni grabbed a broom and shooed Avery up the stairs. At the sound of her voice, the birds peeped and flapped their wings.

"Someone left them at the shelter last week," Toni continued. "I've been feeding them, so they think I'm their mother."

Leona shook her head. "This is too weird." She backed toward the stairs and stepped right into a pile of bird droppings beside Mortimer's old cage. "Oh, yuck!" She hopped around and tried to shake the stuff off her foot.

"Don't you ever clean down here?"

"Yes, we do," said Bruno. "Every day, in fact. You're just lucky that I'm giving you runts the night off tonight."

"Hmph!" said Leona, as she stomped up the stairs.

"Well, she's seen the basement," whispered Meghan, as they followed Leona, "and nothing really went wrong!"

"*AAAIIIGGGHHH!*" screamed Leona from the top of the stairs. She waved her arms wildly. She crashed into the wall. She clawed at the huge bird clinging to her shoulder.

"Mortimer! No!" yelled Toni. She ran up and tried to grab Mortimer.

"He's biting my ear! Help me! Get him off! Get him *off!*" Leona shrieked.

Chapter 9

BIG BIRDS AND LITTLE EARRINGS

Toni pulled Mortimer off Leona's shoulder and tossed him into the living room. Leona covered her ears and sat on the kitchen floor with tears in her eyes.

"Let me see," said Bruno, as he tried to pull Leona's hands away from her head.

Leona slowly let go of her ears. There weren't any marks, but one of her earrings was gone.

While Meghan searched the kitchen floor, Toni looked for Mortimer. She found him on the bookshelf. He was grinding his beak and making smacking noises with his tongue.

Toni held out her hand, and Mortimer spat out a shiny gold lump. Leona's earring. He had crushed it — even the post was bent.

Bruno wrapped his arms around Duke and pulled him off the couch. "I don't think she likes it here, kid." Duke yawned as he rolled onto the floor.

Toni wiped the earring on her shirt. "She's not used to animals, I guess."

Back in the kitchen, she handed the crushed earring to Leona.

"Well...um...at least you weren't hurt," said Toni.

"He tried to *bite* me!" Leona was still on the floor, holding her ear. Avery was rubbing up against her back.

Toni shook her head. "Leona, he thought your earring was a tick. He was chewing it off for you. That's what birds do when they groom each other."

Mortimer flew into the kitchen and landed on the counter. He peeked over the edge and whistled at Leona.

Leona covered her ears and glared at Mortimer. Suddenly, the front door crashed open and Toni's father hurried in. He had an old shoebox tucked under his arm.

"Bring your friends along, Antonina. They can watch what we do!" A rustling sound and a loud 'pee-yah, pee-yah' came from inside the box.

Toni and Meghan followed him downstairs. Leona frowned and stood in the doorway. But when Duke wagged his tail and trotted toward her, she bolted down the stairs.

Toni's father carefully opened the box. Huddled in the corner was a bird the size of a blue jay. It was dark brown with white speckles, and it was holding its left foot close to its belly.

"A nighthawk!" said Toni. "And it has a cut on its leg."

Toni's father smiled. "That's right. You go ahead, Antonina. I think you're ready."

Toni took a deep breath and nodded. While her father held the nighthawk still, Toni cleaned the cut with disinfectant. Then she bandaged the leg with gauze and tape so it could heal without getting infected. After checking that the nighthawk didn't have any other injuries, she put it in a clean cage.

"Good job, Antonina. He'll be fine in a few days."

"Look! He's walking!" said Meghan.

"Leona, you're the newest one here," said Toni's father. "Would you like to feed this little guy his dinner?"

"I guess so."

Toni ran to the freezer and pulled out two glass jars. She sprinkled a spoonful from each jar into a bowl. She gave Leona the bowl and a pair of tweezers.

"Set the bowl in his cage," said Toni. "Then feed him with the tweezers until he starts eating from the bowl by himself."

Leona carefully picked up a brown lump and put it in the bird's mouth. "What is this, anyway?" she asked.

Toni hesitated. "It's...um...freeze-dried mosquitoes and flying ants."

"Yuck!" Leona jumped away from the cage and dropped the tweezers.

Meghan laughed. "What did you think he'd eat? Donuts?"

"I never thought about it, I guess."

"Nighthawks need a lot of food," said Toni. "They can eat over 500 mosquitoes a day." She bent down to get the tweezers, but Leona had already picked them up.

Leona chose another brown lump and carefully put it in the tiny bird's mouth.

Meghan looked over at Toni and smiled. Maybe, thought Toni, this sleepover won't be so bad after all.

After the nighthawk had learned to eat out of the bowl, they went upstairs. Toni's father pulled on his big coat and waved. "I'll be back soon. I'm picking up your mother and the groceries."

"Your dad's nice," said Leona, watching him go. Then she turned to Toni and asked, "Where's your bathroom?"

"At the end of the hall."

When Leona left the kitchen, Meghan patted Toni on the back. "She liked the nighthawk," Meghan said. "So you can stop worrying now."

Bruno pulled Avery off the side of the fish tank and dropped him on the floor. He grinned at Toni. "You can start worrying again."

"Why?"

"*AAAIIIGGGHHH!*" Leona screamed.

"Because there's a goose in the bathtub."

Chapter 10

SHE'LL BE BACK

"*What* goose?" Toni yelled, as she ran down the hall.

"The one that came into the shelter today," called Bruno. "It only has one leg, and they've asked us to keep it for the weekend. If you'd read Dad's emails once in a while, you'd know these things."

Toni opened the bathroom door.

Leona was standing on the toilet. She was hollering at the top of her lungs and swinging the toilet brush at the goose.

The huge bird hopped back and forth in front of Leona. Its long black neck was stretched out and its wings were spread open. Every time Leona moved, the bird hissed and snapped its beak.

"What *is* it?" screamed Leona.

"A Canada goose," said Toni. "He, um...he thinks

you're invading his territory."

Leona jumped off the toilet and ran out the open door. The goose tried to chase her, but it tripped on the bath mat and slid across the floor.

Bruno peeked into the bathroom. "Dad put him in the tub, but I guess he's decided the whole bathroom is his."

Toni looked at Leona. Her hair was in knots, her nylons were ripped and her dress was covered with feathers.

"He's awful," Leona muttered.

"Imagine what he'd be like with *two* legs!" Bruno laughed.

At the sound of Bruno's voice, the goose hopped into the hall.

"Stop him," Leona shrieked. She backed away from the bird and waved the toilet brush in the air.

Bruno laughed. "Let's get him into the tub. Mom and Dad will be home soon." Toni and Bruno talked softly to the goose and guided it back into the bathroom. It hissed and lunged at them, but finally hopped into the tub and settled down on the blankets.

Toni and Meghan looked for Leona. She was standing by the front door with her suitcase.

"I'm going home," she said.

As Leona zipped up her coat, Toni tried to figure out what to say. Her hands felt shaky and her heart pounded. The silence seemed to last forever.

Leona turned her boot upside down and scowled. Avery tumbled out. "Doesn't this bother you? It's like living in a zoo."

Toni stuffed her hands in her pockets so Leona wouldn't see them shaking. She took a deep breath.

"My mom and dad have always worked in animal shelters so we've always had animals around. I just got used to it, I guess."

Leona pulled on her boots. "This place is *weird*."

"It isn't weird, Leona. It's just...different from what you're used to." Toni swallowed hard. She didn't want to cry.

"Goodbye," said Leona, as she walked out the door.

Toni watched Leona walk down the porch steps, then she shut the door.

"Leona decided to leave, did she?" asked Bruno, as he pulled the TV remote out from under Duke's foot.

Toni nodded. "She's going to run home and call all her friends and tell them what a stupid house we live in."

Bruno looked out the front window and then dropped down onto the couch.

"Maybe not," he said. "I think she'll be back."

Toni sighed and wiped the bird fluff off the TV screen with her sleeve. "No, she won't. She's really mad."

Bruno blew dog hair off the remote and turned on the TV. "She'll be back."

"No. She said this was the weirdest house she'd ever seen."

"She'll be back."

"Oh, Bruno, how would *you* know?"

"The neighbor's cat just got another bird. Leona's chasing it down the street."

Meghan ran to the window. Toni pulled open the door as Leona stumbled up the driveway. She held a tiny bird in her hands. There were bloodstains on her coat and tears streaming down her cheeks. "I think it's still alive!" she cried.

Chapter 11

REAL FRIENDS

Leona held out the tiny bird. Its eyes were wide and it was shaking. There was blood on its head and wings.

Leona sobbed as Bruno took the bird and quickly checked its wounds.

"Well, I thought for sure it would be dead, but it just has some cuts and bruises."

"Then why is there so much blood?" asked Leona.

"One of the cuts is across the top of its head," said Toni. "Head wounds bleed a lot — even when they aren't very deep."

"Come on, runts," Bruno said.

Toni, Meghan and Leona followed Bruno downstairs. He set the bird on a towel while Toni got the cotton balls and disinfectant.

Leona wiped the tears off her face and unzipped her

coat. "I thought birds flew south for the winter."

"Not all of them," said Toni. "Some stay behind because they're too old or sick to fly that far, and some stay here all winter on purpose."

Bruno held the bird while Toni gently washed the cuts with disinfectant.

"What kind of bird is it?" asked Leona.

Bruno rolled his eyes. "Don't you know *anything*?" He picked up the bird and set it in a clean cage.

"It's a male song sparrow," said Toni. "Not everyone knows what they look like, Bruno."

Leona smiled at Toni.

"How long will you keep him here?" Meghan asked, as she brushed stray feathers off her jeans.

"Until the cuts heal up. It depends on how healthy he is, really."

Leona peered into the cage. "Could I, um...could I come and see him again sometime?"

Meghan blew the dust off her glasses. "If you stay for dinner, you can see him again tonight."

When they went upstairs, Toni's parents were in the kitchen. Bags of groceries were scattered across the counter. Toni's mother smiled. "Hi, kids. There was a suitcase in the driveway, so I put it in Toni's room."

"Thanks, Mom. It's Leona's."

Leona followed Toni into her room. She opened her suitcase and pulled out a brush. Duke crouched down and snuck across the floor toward the open suitcase.

"*My* parents would never have a place like this." Leona winced as she tried to brush the knots out of her hair.

Toni nodded. Leona's basement was a huge rec room with a TV as big as a couch. At her sleepover, they'd been allowed to go down there, but only if they didn't touch anything or mess around.

"The birds are kind of a family hobby." Toni sat down on her bed and moved the suitcase away from Duke. "We work in the Bird Care Center every day. What do you do with your parents?"

"Nothing, I guess." Leona watched as Duke crawled to her suitcase and tried to stick his nose inside. "My mom and dad are out almost every night, and my babysitter just watches old movies."

"Sounds boring," said Toni, pushing Duke away and holding the suitcase shut with her foot.

Leona straightened her dress and slowly pulled off the last few feathers.

"I get lonely sometimes." She sat down beside Toni. "I guess you have more fun here, but it's so...*weird*. No one else's house is like this."

"It's just different, Leona." Toni took a deep breath. "Give it a chance. It *has* to be better than watching old movies."

Leona chewed her lip. She pulled her suitcase away from Duke and slipped it under the bed. "You're lucky, you know," she said. "You have friends."

Toni stared at Leona. "But...you have friends. You have lots of friends. Everyone listens to you."

"It's not the same thing. You have a real friend. Meghan sticks up for you. She never talks about you behind your back."

Leona is jealous of me? thought Toni. She's the most popular girl in the class!

"Well, I..." Toni didn't know what to say. "Maybe we could be friends. If you could just be a bit more, well...nice."

Leona looked hard at Toni. She tilted her head to one side. Then her face softened. "I guess I could try."

Just then, Meghan walked in with Avery curled up in her arms. "Dinner time!" she said with a grin.

When they reached the kitchen, Toni stopped and stared. Boxes of pizza, bottles of soda and huge bowls of peaches and blueberries crowded the table.

"Wow!" said Leona.

Toni grinned at her father. He'd fooled her all along!

"Sit! Sit!" said Toni's mother. "Eat quickly before Mortimer wakes up!"

As Toni sat in her chair, she heard the click-click-click of bird claws on the kitchen floor. Too late, she thought. Everything had been going just right. *This* could be the worst disaster of all!

Chapter 12

MORTIMER LIKES YOU!

As Leona bit into her pizza, Duke trotted into the kitchen. The gold scrunchie hung from his mouth.

"Duke, drop it!" said Toni.

Duke dropped the scrunchie in Leona's lap and crawled under the table.

Meghan squirmed in her seat and grinned. Duke took up so much room that she had to put her feet on top of him.

Leona gagged as she picked up her scrunchie. It was soaked with dog drool. She started to put it on the table, but changed her mind and dropped it beside her chair. It hit the floor with a splat.

"Oh, Leona, I'm sorry about your...OUCH!" Toni winced. Mortimer was pulling himself up her jeans with his sharp beak and claws.

When he reached Toni's placemat, he yawned, stretched and flapped his wings. A bright blue feather rolled across the table.

"Are we keeping you awake?" Meghan asked.

Mortimer ignored her and walked across the table toward Leona.

Bruno laughed. "Hey, what do you know? I think Mortimer's found a new girlfriend!"

Mortimer stood beside Leona's placemat and hopped from one foot to the other.

Leona pushed her chair away from the table and covered her only earring with her hand. "Why is he doing that?"

"He wants to be friends," said Toni.

Leona raised her eyebrows at Toni. "But he chewed up my earring."

Mortimer turned his back to Leona and peeked over his shoulder. He spread his tail feathers open and shook them.

Meghan laughed. "He likes you! He's showing off!"

Mortimer walked to the edge of Leona's plate and bobbed his head.

"He *must* like you," said Bruno. "He never does that with me!"

Leona smiled and pulled her chair closer to the table. Mortimer bounced from one foot to the other and leaned toward her plate.

"What does he want? My pizza?"

"Try a piece and see," said Meghan, reaching for the

blueberries.

"No way!"

Toni took a deep breath. "He's fun, Leona," she said. "Give him a chance."

"Oh, all right." Leona cut off a piece of pizza and dropped it on the table. Mortimer picked it up with his foot and ate it while he stood on the other leg.

When he had finished the pizza, Mortimer licked off his foot and stared at Leona.

"He likes it!" Leona pulled off a slice of pepperoni and held it in the palm of her hand. Mortimer gently held her thumb with one foot while he nibbled the pepperoni.

"Still think this place is weird?" whispered Meghan.

"It isn't weird, Meghan. It's just different!" Leona smiled at Toni. "My mom won't let me have pets. She says they...Oh!" She shook the water off her arm as Bruno fished Avery out of the aquarium. "She says they make too much mess," she continued with a grin.

She brushed a blue feather off her plate, then offered a string of melted cheese to Mortimer.

"I wish I had pets. This is fun."

This *is* fun, thought Toni. Even if there *is* a goose in the bathtub!

Suddenly, Toni's father smiled and stood up. "I almost forgot. I bought ice cream today! Would you girls like some when you're done your pizza?"

"Yes, please!" said Toni.

"Me too, please!" said Meghan.

Leona didn't answer. She was too busy feeding blueberries to Mortimer.

—

Toni's father laughed and poured himself a cup of coffee.

"Hey, Dad," said Toni. "Don't forget to pour some for Mortimer." She grinned. "You know he just isn't himself without his coffee."

A message from the author:

If you enjoyed *Sleepover Zoo*, I'd be incredibly grateful if you posted a quick review on Amazon. Even a review of only a few sentences is a great help! And if you have any questions, you can reach me at **brenda@brendakearns.com**. Thank you!

Made in the USA
San Bernardino, CA
20 November 2017